The Prince and I

MAYUMI CRUZ

FOREWORD

Welcome to a world where myth and romance intertwine, where the Tamawo of Philippine mythology comes alive in tales that will enchant and captivate you.

Romancing the Tamawo, presented by the 2nd Pinoy Indie Authors Collab, is more than just a collection of short stories; it's a celebration of Filipino storytelling and creativity.

The Tamawo are more than just mythological creatures with their elf-like appearance and shape-shifting talents. They are symbols of the beauty of nature and the force of love. You will see their captivating beauty, their ferocious defense of the natural world, and their happily ever afters when they fall in love with mortals in these pages.

In this Collab, you will find seven unique voices, each weaving a tapestry of love, magic, and mystery. From the depths of enchanted forests to the bustling streets of modern cities, the Tamawo takes center stage, captivating hearts and minds with their mystic charm. Every tale serves as a tribute to the rich fabric of Philippine mythology and the timeless ability of love to overcome obstacles and defy fate.

We invite you to sit back, relax, and immerse yourself in the world of the Tamawo.

\- Mayumi Cruz
Facilitator, Pinoy Indie Authors Collab

**The 2nd Pinoy Indie Authors Collab:
Romancing the Tamawo**

7 Pinoy Authors. 7 Books. 1 Theme.

**"The Prince & I" by Mayumi Cruz
"Dimensional Eclipse" by Maita Rue
"Scent Keeper" by Marigold Andres Uy
"Marahuyo" by Elizabeth Galit
"Till Then, My Tamawo" by Paola Aliedo
"Hearts and Melodies" by Yeyet Soriano
"Lost in Love" by Fred Figueroa**

CONTENTS

ACKNOWLEDGMENTS

My deepest, sincere gratitude goes to my co-authors in this Collab:

Maita, Yeyet, Gold, Pau, Fred, and Beth

for your cooperation and support in making this Collab a successful one.

To more books!

.

1

Anna

THE ZONE

His lips taste slightly sweet with a mild earthy flavor. Much like the water from a natural spring near a river.

I savor the freshness of summer blooms, the splendor of the cold breeze.

I am both lost, and found, in the passion of his kiss.

When our lips part, I sigh, at once longing for more.

We are lying side by side on a majestic bed, limbs tangled in silk sheets, a testimony to a night of unbridled desire.

My hands splay over his broad, chiseled chest. I stare in awe at this beautiful man.

My beautiful man.

His smooth, pale, sparkling skin glitters like crystals touched by the sun. His long, silver white hair is tied in a messy man bun, a few wisps framing his youthful square face.

And his eyes. *His eyes.* Shaped by thick, long lashes, they are orbs of liquid platinum, bright and mesmerizing.

Eyes that are already hungrily raking all over my body again, drinking in my bare skin.

"Anna. . . you're mine, and I am yours," he murmurs, his breath hot and urgent.

My fingers dance over his racing heart in anticipation. I smile as I close my eyes, waiting for his imminent kiss.

But no kiss came.

Frowning, I open my eyes and gasp out loud.

Where is my beautiful man?

The man before me is *not* the man I've spent the night with.

His eyes are white, without color. *Unseeing.*

His skin is ashen and rough. *Cold and hard to my touch.*

He is unmoving. *Lifeless.*

Like a statue.

And then, I watch in horror as suddenly, the statue crumples into dust, leaving no trace of the beautiful man that it was.

I scream, and scream, and scream.

2

Anna

BREAK THE THREE, SET US FREE

"ANNA! ANNA!"

Abruptly, I become aware of Dad shaking my shoulders, anxiously peering at my face.

"D-dad? What happened?" I ask, though I already knew the answer.

"You zoned out again, Anna. We were just talking. Then your face and eyes went blank, and you became still as a corpse."

I cradle my head with my hands, my breath coming in gasps. *I haven't been screaming?* But I heard myself scream, long and loud.

Or did I?

It was all so vivid, so real. I saw it all, heard it all... *felt it all.*

I can still taste his kiss, his lips all over my body. I heard the sound of his beating heart. I touched his smooth, warm skin. I stared at his bright, smoldering eyes.

Before every part of him turned to stone and disintegrated.

"Anna…"

"I-I'm fine, Dad," I try to smile, lifting my face to his. "Don't worry. I'm okay."

He shakes his head. "I don't think these zoning out bouts of yours are okay anymore. They're getting longer. You've been gone for five minutes."

"F-five minutes?" My heart thumps inside my chest. I haven't zoned out for longer than one minute in the past.

"Yes. I've been trying to wake you up for five minutes. You were just sitting there, staring back at me. Unblinking and unmoving."

I shrug, trying to make light of the situation. "Well, maybe I just need more sleep." I don't want to add to his problems. He has enough of them already.

"Anna. . . what did you see? Did you talk to your mother again?"

Dad and I both turn toward the bed. Mom lay there, her blank eyes staring up at the ceiling.

She isn't moving. She hasn't moved from that position since two weeks ago.

She is catatonic.

"Did your mother say the same words as before? Or did she say more?" Dad asks, this time more urgently.

I swallow hard. "Yes, it's the same, Dad. No, she didn't say more." Dad sighs heavily and walks toward the bed, sitting on a chair beside Mom. He picks up her hand and kisses it tenderly.

My heart aches at the scene before me, but without a little guilt. I hate lying to my father. I always tell him I see Mom in my daydreams whenever I zone out.

Which is true — *but only for the first time.*

***

That very first time I zoned out, my mother and I were walking on the beach, facing the Castle of Qwajo. She turned to me, took my hands, and pressed them to her heart. Then, slowly, she vanished into thin air, leaving me with an epiphany that echoed in my ears before it dissolved with the wind:

"Break the three, set us free."

Since then, Dad and I have had numerous discussions about that enigmatic statement. What was Mom trying to tell me? She didn't say 'tree': I'm positive she said 'three,' the number. Three—what three? Three things? What things? And from where are we to be set free?

Truth be told, the only thing I'd like to be set free from is this depressing poverty in the Kingdom of Qwajo.

As far as I can remember, it has always been like this in our tiny island kingdom, situated in the middle of the Visayan Sea.

According to our history books, the Kingdom of Qwajo was granted autonomy and declared a separate sovereign country by the Philippine government out of fear for its first king.

King Leroy was rumored to be a powerful sorcerer who built the Castle of Qwajo and established the kingdom, which was comprised of people who came from the surrounding islands. He was a wise and just king who ruled over his kingdom and led them to great wealth and prosperity.

Which is a joke.

Because at present, Queen Sonya, the direct descendant of King Leroy, is sick and dying. She hasn't been seen since . . . I don't know, years? Her husband, King Treo, is dead. Their irresponsible son, the Crown

Prince Liam–that self-entitled, lazy, fat bum–is gallivanting somewhere in the world.

And the current Regent, Duke George, the Queen's cousin, is an absent steward who prefers to stay inside the comforts of the Castle instead of checking into the people's welfare. He is an idiot who doesn't have any desire or powers—sorcery or otherwise—to improve the living conditions of the citizens of Qwajo.

No, there is no magic in the Kingdom of Qwajo. There never has. We are normal, boring people ruled by an incompetent monarchy that should have been abolished decades ago.

The way I see it, Qwajo should not have separated itself from the Philippine government. Maybe we would have been better off on the mainland.

Because in Qwajo, jobs are scarce. Food is scarce. Business is scarce. Opportunities are scarce.

But for some reason, Qwajonians are content being like this. No one has attempted to leave the island to seek better opportunities on the mainland. Because, seriously, leave with what? With empty pockets?

Qwajonians have stayed put here. Maybe they are afraid of whatever awaits them in an unknown world. Maybe the hopelessness of the kingdom's situation has seared into their bones and imprisoned them into inertia.

Sad to say, I am one of them.

***

"Break the three, set us free."

My mother's words are as confounding as the illness that abruptly took over her.

When we woke up one morning two weeks ago, Dad and I were shocked to find her in this condition. She cannot talk, walk, or speak. She just laid there, her eyes locked on the ceiling. She's like a living dead.

I've lost count of how many times we tried to wake her up, solicit any reaction from her, get her to move, or speak. But up to this day, she hasn't responded.

Dad has been inconsolable. I can hear him weeping silently every night. Mom's condition has not only affected our family. It has also affected Dad in more ways than one. He has neglected our pitiful business: a small pawnshop—not that it has many customers to begin with—to take care of Mom.

Every time I see Dad bathing my mother, brushing her hair, changing her clothes, feeding her, and attending to her personal needs, my heart breaks into pieces. He loves her so much.

I try to help, but Dad insists it's his job as a husband to care for his wife. So, instead, I tend the store, cook for them, and help with other chores.

What else can I do? There is no job for me outside our pawnshop business. I've been looking for work ever since I finished my legal management course, and I haven't found one.

Presently, Dad is saying, his brows knitted in deep thought, "Anna, do you think those words uttered by your mother whenever you zone out are the cure to her illness?"

I bite my lip guiltily. Dad doesn't know that the next bouts of zoning out were not of my mother anymore.

They were of that beautiful man, with moments of heated, intimate passion that would have made him cringe in embarrassment.

"I don't know, Dad," I reply, pushing my dirty thoughts away, hoping my father doesn't notice my blushing cheeks. I walk up to him, standing by his side as

I stare sadly at my mother. "I told you before, I'm as puzzled as you are."

"But when she said, 'Break the three,' it sounded like a curse, don't you think?"

Here we go again.

"Dad," I groan. "There is no such thing as curses and magic here in Qwajo."

"I'm not saying there is." His denial is immediate. He knows I'm pissed at any talk about magic, curses, or sorcerers—aside from the monarchy. "It's just that. . . I'm exploring all possibilities, you know. I really hope she could have said more to help us understand what she's trying to convey."

"I'm sure she will. When I zone out again," I say playfully.

"No, Anna!" He stood up, knocking down his chair.

For a moment, I am taken aback by my father's reaction. He's always been calm, even in extreme distress. This is the first time—ever—I've seen him out of control.

"Don't say that! If it were up to me, I don't want you to zone out again. Ever! I don't want you to be like your mother!"

"Dad!" I gasp. "I'm not ending up like Mom, okay?"

"How would you know? You're zoning out more and more these days, and they're getting longer. It isn't normal anymore. I'm not losing you, too, Anna. I'm not losing both of my girls!"

His normally jovial, handsome face is lined with worry and fear. His brown eyes, so like mine, are wide with panic. Exhaustion and depression over Mom's condition are taking their toll on my poor father.

"Dad," I force my voice lower to calm him. "I don't like to zone out, either, believe me. I was just trying to lighten us up. And please stop thinking about me ending up like Mom. Worrying and overthinking won't help solve our situation."

His shoulders slump, and he exhales tiredly. "I-I'm sorry, sweetheart. Maybe I'm just tired. I haven't been sleeping well lately. I keep thinking of ways to wake your mother up, and my mind always comes back to the words she told you."

I sigh. "Dad, we can't put all our hopes for Mother's healing into something that we're not even sure what it is. For all we know, it's just a product of my imagination."

Dad stares at me intensely, and I am again taken aback, this time, by the fierce conviction I see in him.

"I don't think so, Anna. For some reason, your mom cannot speak, but she communicates through your daydreams. She's trying to tell us something. I know it in my bones."

Before I can reply to Dad, we hear a guttural sound from the bed. We both look. Our eyes widen in shock as we see Mom's head turned toward us, her black eyes fixed upon us. Then she opens her mouth, and, in a clear, steady voice, she utters a single word.

"*One.*"

Dad and I both jump when the doorbell to the pawnshop downstairs rings.

3

Anna

THE MISSING OWL SCULPTURE

"You're joking, right?"

"Do I look like I'm joking?"

The tall, thin man is sitting stiffly in front of me. His flat, dead eyes, set in deep sockets, stare unblinkingly at me.

He's right. He isn't joking. In fact, I don't think he has joked even once in his lifetime.

Cirilo Salamanca is the man who rang the doorbell to our pawnshop ten minutes ago, when my mother had a brief moment of lucidness before sliding back to her catatonic state in the blink of an eye.

I have come down to the pawnshop to attend to the unexpected caller. I left my father upstairs, laughing and crying at the same time, his hope rekindled.

But I'm not my father, and I'm not feeling hopeful.

I'm feeling uneasy.

And when an unexpected visitor arrives to offer me a job, promising a compensation that's too good to be true, I get more tense and not a little bit suspicious.

"Mr. Salamanca, let me get this straight: You're not pawning anything, but you want to employ my services to find your antique sculpture, which was stolen from you, and you're willing to pay me half a million pesos to find it?"

"Correct."

"But I'm not a private investigator, Mr. Salamanca. I'm just helping out my father in this pawnshop until I find a job."

"Then you're in luck. This is a job I'm offering you."

"Even without any background as an investigator?"

"How hard can it be to search for an object? It only requires diligence and persistence. Some analytical skills, of course. I'm sure you have all those qualities. Plus, the pay I'm offering is a hundred times bigger."

He has a point. Still. . .

"Miss Chavez, all you have to do is find my sculpture, and you'll be five hundred thousand pesos richer. With that amount of money, you can take your parents out of here. You can move to the mainland. You can live in moderate luxury. And your mother can get the best medical attention."

I glare at him. "How did you know about that?"

"Everyone in this place knows about your mother. I heard them talking."

I'm still not convinced. "Tell me again how you ended up here? And why can't you tell me who is the client you're representing?"

He exhales, the only sign that shows he's annoyed. "Look, if you don't want the job, just say so. I don't need to be grilled. But I'm telling you, this is your only chance to give your parents and yourself a better life. Take it or leave it."

He starts to leave.

A chance to get out of this place. Who could resist that?

"Wait, Mr. Salamanca. Do you have a photo of your sculpture?"

His mouth twitches. "Yes, I have. Here."

He places a photo on top of the glass shelf between us.

I blanch.

"This!? You want me to find this?"

"Yes."

"You do know that this sculpture is the symbol of our kingdom, right?" I ask incredulously, pointing at the photo of the white owl sculpture. "This mass-produced stonework is in every citizen's home! Are you saying that I have to march into each house and inspect every owl sculpture to see if it's stolen?"

He looks at me intently before replying in a monotone, "This one is different."

"How can this be different?" I pick up the photo with one hand. "It's the same! Look, same image, same color, same. . ."

I pause, stopping in mid-sentence.

Am I seeing things, or did the owl's golden eyes just *blinked* at me?

"You were saying?"

"I. . Did . . . did you see that?" I croak, reeling from shock.

"What?"

"Y-you didn't see that?"

"See what?" He exhales again, this time more forcefully. "Miss Chavez, let's not waste each other's time. Take the job, and I will give you a downpayment of ten thousand pesos. Right here, right now."

My mouth drops open. I am mind-blown. He's paying me ten thousand pesos *now?* I haven't even found the missing object! What if I don't find it?

As if reading my mind, he adds, "If you don't find the owl, you don't have to give the money back to me. It's yours to keep."

Wow. I should be jumping for joy at this stranger's kindness.

But there's something that's not quite right. Something's bothering me about him. It's almost as if he's trying *too hard* to get me to accept the job. Why?

And what about the sculpture blinking at me? Did that really happen? Why didn't he see it?

I look again at the photo. The owl stared right back at me.

Unblinking.

My brows curl. *It must have been my imagination.*

"Are you taking the job, or not?" Mr. Salamanca carefully places ten one-thousand-peso bills in front of me, without waiting for an answer. Maybe because he already knew my answer.

We need the money desperately, and desperate times call for desperate measures.

I nod wordlessly, wondering how on earth I am going to find an owl sculpture that looks like every other owl sculpture in every home in our kingdom.

A ghost of a smile flits over Mr. Salamanca's face as a mischievous gleam sparks into his eyes when I pick up the money.

"Thank you, Miss Chavez. I only ask that once you've found the statue, call me immediately using this phone," he instructs me as he hands me a cell phone. "There's only one number there, and it's mine."

"Of course," I mutter as I reach for the phone.

But he doesn't let go of the phone easily. Puzzled, I lift my eyes to him.

He stares back with his black, dead eyes for a moment, before letting me have the phone. "And don't worry, Miss Chavez. *The owl will find you.* Not the other way around."

4

Anna

THE OWL

SHAPED LIKE AN OWL, THE ISLAND KINGDOM OF QWAJO IS mostly surrounded by steep limestone cliffs of varying heights rising from the sea.

The highest point of the island is on the northernmost part, where the dilapidated medieval-style Castle of Qwajo stands. It is surrounded by a wide moat, with a concrete drawbridge connecting it to the rest of the island.

The citizens of Qwajo dwell in the western and eastern regions of the island. With a population of roughly fifteen-thousand, Qwajo has only one city. Unlike the castle, the city has concrete roads, establishments, and residences scattered all over the hilly land, though most, if not all, are in various states of disrepair.

Qwajo is comparable to the island country of Malta in southern Europe—only smaller and definitely poorer.

Beyond the city, there is a rolling terrain with a lush forest and a flowing river leading to the southernmost region, where the white sand beach meets the Visayan Sea.

I've thought long and hard about where to start looking for the owl sculpture. There's this antique shop that houses priceless objects like paintings and sculptures purportedly dating back to ancient times. There's also this quaint gallery that exhibits artwork by penniless artists. And yes, there's always the plan to knock on every door and take a peek into their homes.

But my feet have brought me here.

The Seaside Night Market is located at the westernmost tip of the island on a grassy knoll leading to a cliff overlooking the sea.

Some twenty or more Qwajonians are there, selling used and second-hand wares: impoverished sellers who are hoping to dispose of their precious things in exchange for a small amount of money from equally impoverished buyers.

I look up at the night sky. It's a full moon, and the sea breeze is cold. A perfect night for an evening stroll.

If I find the owl tonight, it would be more than perfect.

There aren't too many buyers inside. Understandable, since it's a Wednesday and payday is still two days away. As expected, there are also sellers offering white owl sculptures.

I move from one stall to the next, ignoring the sellers' calls, glancing at the photo of Mr. Salamanca's owl sculpture on my cell phone from time to time.

I don't know why, but I don't see an owl statue that piques my interest, though they all look the same. I just pass by the stalls and glance at the items for sale.

When I reach the farthest end of the tent, I turn around, trace my way back to where I came from, and walk around the stalls again.

Back and forth, I wander around. Aimlessly.

I am looking, but I'm not really looking. I know it doesn't make sense, but I feel compelled to follow where my feet take me.

On the third time I reach the farthest end, I suddenly stop and frown at what I see.

Some three meters outside the tent, illuminated by the moonlight, a stone well with a wooden roof stands.

I don't remember there being a stone well with a wooden roof moments ago.

Against my better judgment, I walk toward it. Beside it, there is a small table with numerous owl statues on display.

"Good evening, Miss."

The sudden appearance of the seller beside me startles me. He is a tall man, wearing a hooded jacket and jeans. I can't quite see his face. His head is covered by the hood, and he's wearing dark glasses. I don't think I've seen him around.

Who wears dark glasses at night? Unless he's blind.

As if confirming my thoughts, two white Siberian huskies appear on both sides of the man, silently sitting on the ground.

I take a step back.

"Don't be afraid, Miss," the man says. "My dogs are friendly. Do you see anything you want? I have a collection of rare items."

His deep but soft voice makes me feel at ease. I walk around his table. "Strange. I've not seen this stall before."

"Hmm. Strange, indeed. I've been here for two weeks now, waiting for you. . . I mean, buyers like you."

"Really? But I'm just window-shopping. I don't know what to get for now."

"Let me help you." He picks an owl statue from among the others on the table and hands it to me. "I think you'd like this one, Miss."

I start to refuse his offer. But when I look down at the owl in his hands, its eyes suddenly come to life. They begin to glow brightly—and they *blink repeatedly* at me.

I gasp and grab the owl from him. "I. . . I'll take this. How much is this?"

"It's only one hundred pesos, Miss."

I can't believe my luck. I have found the statue, and it only costs me a hundred pesos!

I pay him hastily. As I start to leave, clutching the statue in my hands, he stops me.

"Miss," he whispers, "please be careful. Two men are hiding behind two stalls from here. They've been following you. No, don't turn around," he warns me. "They'll know you're into them."

I frown. "How did you see them? You're blind."

He grins lazily. "I never said I was." He taps the dogs' heads, who let out a low growl. "I suggest you make a run for it toward the cliff. My dogs and I will try to distract them."

5

Anna

DANGER

I'VE BEEN RUNNING FOR ALMOST TEN MINUTES NOW, AND I still don't see anyone following me. I stop, catching my breath.

Looking around, I see that I'm almost at the edge of the cliff, far away from the night market.

Have I been duped into believing that vendor?

I didn't really stop to think about the truth of his words. When he'd told me to run, I did just that. I didn't even look back. I ran as fast as I could toward the cliff.

I'm not normally this gullible. It's just that. . . he seemed an honest and reliable person. And when he smiled at me, I felt I knew him.

Weird, right?

But now, I'm beginning to have doubts.

What if he was just trying to lure me here for his own sinister agenda?

Just then, I hear the sound of a motorcycle. Engine roaring, it is rushing toward me. I squint to see who it is. Two men are on it, and as they get nearer, I see the one in the back has a gun.

Which he fires in succession. . . at me.

My jaw drops open. *What? Why are they firing at me?*

Standing there, unmoving, with a gaping mouth, a bullet hits me on the left shoulder.

I scream in pain, my right hand clutching the wound. But I don't drop the statue. Instead, I hug it tight to my chest. I stagger backward, farther to the edge of the cliff.

They stop a few feet away from me. The second man gets off, his gun still pointing at me.

"Give us the owl," the driver yells at me. "And we'll let you live."

I suck in a breath. *They want the owl? Someone else is after this owl? Why did Mr. Salamanca fail to tell me that very important and very critical fact?*

But my anger and my pain surge inside me, making me bold and stupidly brave. Whatever reason he had for keeping it a secret from me, my rage is fired.

"Liar!" I yell back. "You'll kill me anyway, after I've given you the owl!"

With an evil grin, the man with the gun scoffs, "You're right. So, let's get this over with, shall we?" He points the gun at my head.

I never really knew what happened. One moment I am standing there, and one moment I am hurled backwards by something forceful, something heavy, something on my chest.

I look down at my hands.

That something is the statue. It is *pinning me down* as it suddenly becomes heavy as a boulder, pressing onto my body, forcing me to fall backward and avoid the bullet.

What's happening?!

Wide-eyed, I watch in wonder as the bullet misses me and shoots above my head, before I fall, fall, fall. . . down the cliff . . . into the cold, raging waters below.

When my body hits the water, my last thoughts are of Dad, of Mom, and of my hope for a better life—now gone. I close my eyes, embracing death.

6

Liam

FREE AT LAST

As soon as the seawater touches me, the stone disintegrates, and I unfurl like the wings of a new butterfly, finally freed from its chrysalis.

At last, the spell that bound me to the owl sculpture is broken.

I spring out of the sea and quickly breathe in a generous amount of air, before I dive back into the water, hastily searching for Anna. The trail of blood from the gunshot wound on her shoulder guides me to her. She's unconscious.

I grab her and breathe air into her mouth, and we stay underwater. All the while, my eyes are peeled above us, watchful and waiting, lest those evil men decide to follow us into the water. I need not have worried. After a couple of minutes, they leave.

I swim, dragging Anna along while making sure her head is elevated above the water. I go around the base of the cliff, where tall, narrow, gigantic rocks stand guard. Before going under the rocks, I breathe air into Anna's mouth again. I swim under for a few minutes, with Anna in tow, before I spring out of the water, into a hidden cave I've known since childhood.

This is my home away from home, a single-room dwelling complete with modern facilities and conveniences I need.

I get out of the water, carrying a still unconscious Anna in my arms. I lay her down on the bed. Eyes closed and hands raised, I sit beside Anna and summon my magic, concentrating all my energy on it. It does not fail me. In an instant, the bullet emerges from her left shoulder and drops to the ground. Her open wound closes and heals.

I flick my hand, and her clothes disappear, replaced by a fresh set of clothes under a warm blanket as hot air dries her hair and body. Another flick, and deep sleep descends upon her.

Next, I make a fire to warm us both. Then I turn on the lights scattered all over the place, illuminating the numerous owl sculptures in my vast workroom.

For the very first time in what seems like forever, I allow myself a smile. With the first spell broken, my magic has returned.

But then, my face darkens as I remember that there is much to be done. There are two more spells to break.

Anna moans softly, and I immediately attend to her. The pain must not have receded as quickly as I hoped. My magic still has not regained its full power.

I summon all my strength as I lay my hands above her head, willing the magic to do its thing. After a while, she becomes silent, and the frown on her forehead clears up. I relax, thankful for this small win.

My eyes feast on her beautiful face. Even in repose, I am awed at her delicate beauty. My mother once remarked that she's a dead ringer for Liza Soberano, the actress from the mainland, but I disagree.

Anna is far more beautiful.

I touch her perfectly-shaped face, crowned by long, wavy brown hair. My fingers dance over her smooth, honey-colored skin, her highly-set eyebrows, and curly lashes resting on eyelids that are now closed, covering her brown eyes, her majestic nose, and her red, full lips.

How I've hungered to lay eyes on her again. And now, here she is. At last.

But my anger is inflamed once more when I remember what those two men did to her. My fists clench, and the lights around us flicker wildly, mirroring my emotions.

Those men nearly killed her. When I get out of here, I will hunt them down and kill them.

They will pay dearly for what they did to *my wife*.

7

Anna

A DISCOVERY OF WITCHES

I'm in the zone again. I'm with my beautiful man.

He's touching my cheek tenderly, his lips slightly open. His golden eyes are laden with worry and genuine concern. I feel safe in the love I see there, embracing me like the warmth of a thick, wool cloak.

I frown.

Wait. Why would I feel this if I'm already dead?

I gasp and sit up straight. The sudden movement causes my head to throb immediately, as if hit by a baseball bat. I squeeze my eyes tight. I cradle my head with my hands as I moan in pain.

"Easy. . . you're still weak."

My eyes snap open. I can hear that voice. *I am hearing that voice.* I am not dreaming.

Slowly, I lift my head and come face-to-face with the object of my dreams. *My beautiful man.*

He is real, and he is here with me. Smiling, bare-chested, breathtakingly handsome.

But dreams are different from reality. And the first emotion I feel isn't joy, but fear and uncertainty.

Especially when I look down to see I'm wearing fresh new clothes.

"W-what. . .what happened? Who are you? What did you do to me?" I shriek.

He inhales sharply, his face turning grim, as if my words have angered him. But why? I should be the one angry, shouldn't I?

"I didn't realize how bad it is. . . ," he starts to mutter, but changes his mind. He pulls in a deep breath before replying to me, "I saved you from drowning, and I nursed your wound. I also dried you up and changed your clothes. Don't worry. Your honor is intact, I assure you."

Strange as it is, I believe him. I clear my throat. "Where am I?"

"My workroom. Someone. . . jokingly called this the Owl Cave."

My eyes roam over the place. I am awed. The cave is a mix of natural and synthetic beauty.

It has a dome-shaped, high ceiling, creating a magical, ethereal atmosphere. The walls are smooth, golden-colored limestone, which adds to the cave's enchanting appearance. A serene, natural pool of crystal-clear water shimmers at the center.

On the other side, though, is quite a different view. It looks like a modern apartment with modern furniture and fixtures. It practically screams wealth.

Wealth? No one is this wealthy in Qwajo. And shouldn't there be a door here somewhere? I don't see one.

But when I notice the owl sculptures scattered on the floor, it suddenly hits me. I gasp loudly. "My owl! Did you see the owl I was carrying? I need it! I need to return it to its rightful owner!"

"Return it to its rightful owner?" His brows rise up.

"Yes!" I said, spreading my hands, trying to make him understand my predicament.

He is smiling at me—humorously, but nonetheless, infuriatingly.

"I was hired to find it. If I don't return it, I won't get the money. My family needs the money so we can get out of this miserable island and my mother can be treated. . . *wait!*" I jerk to a stop, my eyes large as saucers.

"Since when have I been here?" I ask tremulously.

He smoothly answers, "Last night."

"What?!" I get out of the bed, ignoring my momentary dizziness, and stand up. "I have to go! My Dad, my Mom, she's sick, they need me! And I have to give the owl to Mr. Salamanca!"

This time, he frowns at me. "Mr. Salamanca?"

"Yes! He's the one who hired me to find the owl," I explain. I look around. "Have you seen the owl I was carrying? Oh, please, please, tell me, you've seen it!"

He crosses his arms across his chest. "Of course I've seen it."

"Where? Where is it?" I'm panicking.

There are so many owl statues here. *Which one of these is my owl?*

He walks toward me and holds my hand, leading me to the pool at the center. His hand is soft, like cotton; it sort of calms me. And when he walks, the lights over our heads touch his skin. It glimmers like diamonds.

If not for my mounting panic, I would have been content to just stare.

He turns to me. "Can you close your eyes?"

"W-what?"

"Close your eyes for a minute, and when you open them, you will see your owl statue on the ground. But then, I want you to put it in the water. Can you do that?"

"Uh. . . why would I put it in the water?"

He smiles enigmatically. "You'll see. Can you do that? Please?"

I am confused, but I find myself saying, "Okay. Yes."

"Good. Now close your eyes."

Dutifully, I obey. When I open them again, I see the owl statue on the ground.

But my beautiful man, though, is nowhere in sight. "Hello? Where are you?" I yell, but my words just echo back at me.

Where did he go? Will I see him again?

I don't even know his name. I feel a sudden, inexplicable sadness at his absence.

Sighing heavily, I pick up the owl and put it into the water. No sooner does it touch the salty water than it crumbles like sand, disappearing under the water.

"No. . . !" hands extended, I start to speak, only to be rendered speechless when slowly, in place of the statue, my beautiful man emerges from the water, smiling at me.

I gape at him, not believing what I have just seen. "What. . . what are you?! Who are you?" I demand, fear piercing my heart.

"I am a Tamawo," he calmly replies, his eyes focused on my face. "And my name is Liam. *Prince* Liam."

Dumbfounded, words rush out of my mouth. "T-tamawo? An encanto? Like those stories from the mainland? No! There's no such thing as encanto, or tamawo, or, magic! *Magic isn't real!* That wasn't magic! I bet you were already under the water, and that. . . that statue, it's probably made of salt or something, and then, then, you. . ."

"Anna. Magic is as real as you and me. You saw it yourself. I *am* that owl statue."

I shake my head empathically. "No! And you are not the prince of Qwajo, either! The prince is an ugly, fat, lazy bastard who's now circling the globe or whatever it is he's doing, just as long as it's not here in Qwajo!"

His brows curl. Then, surprisingly, he chuckles. "That bad, huh? Boy, I have a lot of work cut out for me, don't I?"

"This isn't funny!" I yell louder. My mind is running wild, thinking of my parents. I have been gone since yesterday. Dad could be looking for me, worried sick, on top of my mother's ailment.

"Look, I don't know how you did that trick, or what you're trying to prove, but please let me have my owl and my phone, and I'll be out of your hair!"

Suddenly, I catch sight of my phone lying on the table beside the bed. "My phone!"

I shriek and run toward it, but before I can get to it, the phone floats up and leaps to the bed *by itself.*

"W-what. . . ?!"

I turn around and see him smiling. His right hand is lifted. He flicks it, and the phone suddenly flies off, landing softly on his feet.

The hairs on my arm stand. "Y-you did that?"

In answer, he flicks his hand again, and the phone returns to the bed.

I am dumbfounded. But that doesn't diminish my resolve to get my phone. "Enough of these tricks, please. I just want my phone."

I move to pick it up, but it flies away again, returning to its original location on the table by the side of the bed.

"Stop it," I beg him. "Please let me have my phone."

"Then get it, Anna," he smoothly says.

I blanch. "You know my name?"

"Oh, I know a lot about you, Anna. More than anyone else." He flicks his hand again. The phone flies, landing on the ground at his feet once more.

"How did you know my name?" I bark. "And what did you mean when you said you knew me more than anyone else?"

"Anna, *I know you*. And I know that you're strong-willed and hot-headed."

Despite the fear crawling through me, I can feel my hot anger rising. Especially when he said I'm hot-headed. I refuse to be toyed with, even by this beautiful man of my dreams.

I step toward him, and he lifts his hand again, preparing to flick it. Rage overtakes me as I extend my palm and scream out loud, "I said, STOP IT!"

The phone abruptly lifts from where it was and flies again—*straight to my palm*—before it falls down again.

I gasp loudly. "W-what...?!"

He grins with satisfaction. "You see? Magic is real, Anna. You have it, too."

"H-how?! Why?!"

"Anna. . . *you're a witch*."

***

The phone chimes at that exact moment, indicating a new voice message. Automatically, I click it.

Mr. Salamanca's menacing voice blares to my ear, adding up to the already tangled situation I find myself in.

"Miss Chavez, I know you have the owl. If you want to see your parents alive again, bring it to me at the Castle tonight at exactly midnight. The Duke and I will be waiting for you."

In the background, my mother is shouting. "Anna! Anna! Be careful! Save us!"

"Mom? Is that you?" I shriek, shock reverberating through me at hearing my mother's voice sounding normal. "You're not sick anymore? You're okay now?"

Mom's voice is quickly replaced by Mr. Salamanca's growl. "Tonight at midnight, Anna. Bring the owl!"

The message ends abruptly.

I clasp the phone in my hand tightly as my breath comes out as shaky gasps. I turn to Liam, whose face has become grim.

"I heard."

Tears well up in my eyes. "I. . . I don't understand what's happening. Your magic. *My* magic. My mother. . . the Duke?"

He inhales deeply. "First, tell me about Mr. Salamanca."

I tell him everything. He listens intently, his face growing darker by the second. When I reach the part where I was nearly killed, his jaw is so tautly clenched, it looks like it will snap open.

When I finish talking, he grasps both my hands.

"Anna, Mr. Salamanca is, in fact, Salas, the Warlock. I recognized his voice at once. He helped my uncle, the Duke, in trying to steal Qwajo's source of magic. The Trifecta, consisting of my mother, the Queen, a sorceress, and my father, the King, a Tamawo, and their best friend–*your mother*–a witch, fought against them, using the Power of Three spell."

I am stunned. "Wait. My mother? *A witch?*"

"Yes. Like you. It runs in your family."

As I struggle to wrap my head around the fact that *I* am a witch, that *my mother* is a witch, and that we are *a family of witches,* Liam proceeds to tell me more.

8

Liam

THE POWER OF THREE SPELL AND THE OMNI CURSE

I TELL—NO, *REMIND*—ANNA EVERYTHING, HOPING THAT IN DOING SO, her memory will return. I'm not getting my hopes up too much, though. Mother said everything would come back to her gradually if I did everything right.

The Power of Three spell was cast by Qwajo's Trifecta. Singularly, each has their own powerful magic. Collectively, they are a force to be reckoned with. They protect the kingdom and ensure that its people are safe and thriving.

When my uncle went after the Source of Qwajo's magic to claim the throne, the Trifecta fought against him.

It was supposed to be an easy fight. Uncle George's magic was not innate; it was learned. But they hadn't counted on Warlock, who allied with him. Salas was an evil and formidable opponent who utilized powerful, dark magic in fighting them.

At the moment when Salas had almost defeated them, the Power of Three spell had been the Trifecta's last recourse.

Three spells to overpower all spells and protect the Source of magic from Uncle George and the evil Warlock, which created the *unbreakable Omni Curse to vanquish* them as well.

And it worked. The Source of magic was put to safety. Uncle George was cursed. The Warlock was knocked out and imprisoned in a block of crystalline limestone deep under the Visayan Seabed.

But magic as powerful as that, and cast for the very first time, had come with a high price. It did not only backfire. It went wayward.

The Omni Curse stripped the Trifecta of their powers and incapacitated them.

My mother contracted a terminal illness; my father vanished; and their friend was locked in a state of nothingness. It also dispersed them to separate, unknown locations.

***

At this point, Anna frowns and asks, "But if they are cursed and defeated, how come Mr. Salamanca–*Salas*–came and found me?"

My jaw hardens. "It only means one thing. He has escaped from his prison."

"I thought the Omni Curse was unbreakable?"

"Yes, but it doesn't last long. The duration of the Omni Curse is only ten days. The Trifecta should have finished him off for good after that, if they were here, but. . . as you now know, everything went awry."

"And my mother. . . what happened to her?"

"You mentioned she was sick? I think that was one of the consequences of the curse. But I'm glad your mother still ended up with you and your father, not in some dark place, or with anyone else."

She nods, then frowns again. "They say the King is dead."

"That's not true. If my father is dead, all of us should be dead, too, and Qwajo should have been obliterated from the map. Three spells by three powerful wielders of magic produced the Omni Curse, and if one of them dies, everything is lost. No, my father is not dead. He is missing, and I don't know where he is."

"You said 'one of the consequences.' Are there more?"

I nod, sadly. "Yes. The spell plunged the kingdom into poverty and famine, its vast riches vanishing like the morning mist."

"You mean, Qwajo wasn't like this before?"

"Qwajo is the richest kingdom on Earth, Anna. Richer than Thailand, Brunei, or Luxembourg. Our magic is superior to theirs."

"Magic? They are rich because of magic?"

"How else would you explain their wealth and prosperity?"

She falls silent, no doubt confused by everything I've told her so far. But there is so much more. It's a lot to take in, but it can't be helped.

I know that a part of her doesn't want to believe me, but I'm hoping that a larger and stronger part of her prevails over her doubts.

"But," she asks again, "why can't I or anyone in Qwajo, remember all that? I've always known Qwajo to be impoverished."

"Everyone's memory was wiped out by the Omni Curse, Anna."

"Everyone?"

"Yes. Tell me: do you remember where you were, or anything you've done differently, from before two weeks ago?"

My question throws her off.

"What do you mean? I'm a fresh college graduate, and I've been helping my parents in our pawnshop because I can't find a job."

"Before that, do you remember going to school? What school? Do you have friends? Did you go some place else? Did you do anything else? Do you remember looking for jobs?"

Her brows draw together as she searches her mind for the answers to my questions. The expression on her face tells me she found none.

"You don't, do you? That's because the Omni curse was cast two weeks ago. It erased the memory of every Qwajonian before that day."

She bites her lip, reminiscing. "I've been having dreams even while awake. My mother told me in my dream, 'Break the spell, set us free.' Do you think it has something to do with the Power of Three spell?"

"Yes. That's great!" I reply, happy at the information she shared. "That meant she found a way to communicate with you despite her condition. I think because the same powers run in your blood."

She scoffs. "Up until today, I didn't believe in magic. Much less, that I have magical powers."

"You do, Anna. Your powers enabled you to break the first spell."

"I didn't know I'd broken the first spell. What was the first spell?"

"The Trifecta bound me inside the owl sculpture and hid me. You found me and freed me."

She stares into my eyes. "Where were you? I mean, where was the owl sculpture hidden?"

"I was sent to Kisignan, the realm of the Tamawos, my relatives on my father's side. For safekeeping. After the Omni Curse, my cousin frequented Qwajo, hoping to stumble upon you."

She gasps softly. "The seller at the night market!"

I smile. "Yes. Elro is my cousin. You know him. We all grew up together."

"Really? That's why I feel at ease with him," she mutters. "But why didn't he defend me from the men who almost killed me?"

"The Curse prevents him, and all Tamawos for that matter, from acting for or against anyone in Qwajo. They can only enter and exit Qwajo through the portal, the stone well that you saw, but they're basically onlookers."

"That's too bad," she exclaims, her brows knitted. "Based on what you're telling me, Qwajo needs all the help it can find."

Good. Anna, the thinker, is slowly coming out. She really is a born strategist.

Aloud, I say, "I don't know *when* they will be able to help us. I certainly hope it happens before all three spells are broken. We truly need their help. But the first spell is done, thanks to you."

She purses her lips. "Okay, so, the first spell is broken. I still don't understand how my mother is okay now? I'm sure that was her voice I heard."

My brows curl and I think hard. "I believe that for each spell broken, a member of the Trifecta is released from the consequence of the Curse. That's the only logical explanation for it. First spell broken, first of the Trifecta released."

She nods in understanding. "And the second spell? What is it?"

"I can't tell you that," I say, shaking my head apologetically. "I musn't. Or it won't be broken."

"How about the third?"

I heave a deep breath. "The third spell. . . *I don't remember what it is or how it can be broken.* The Omni Curse wiped out my memory of it. And. . . ," my jaws clench so tightly, my teeth hurt, "I. . I can't remember what the Source of magic is, too."

"*What?* Then, how can the Curse be broken?" She squeals, panic lacing her voice. "It's like we're flying blind!"

"We just have to take one spell at a time," I say calmly. "Eventually, memories will rush in, I'm sure of it. This isn't permanent."

With a whimper, Anna covers her face with her hands, a picture of helplessness.

I wrap my arms around her, whispering, "Ssshh. . . everything will be okay."

After a minute, her shoulder droops, and her body relaxes, molding itself into mine.

I breathe in deeply the sweet scent of her hair. I relish the feel of her soft skin against mine. It's been too long since I've held her close to my heart. Every minute without her has been like an eternity, many times over.

Abruptly, she detaches herself from me, backing away a few steps. Her rejection hits me like a punch in the gut. I want to pull her back in, but I know it isn't the right time yet.

"Okay. I understand," she exhales. "But what am I supposed to do tonight? If I bring you to Mr. Salama—I mean, Salas—he's sure to kill you."

I smile despite the pain I'm feeling. She doesn't want me killed; that's a relief.

"But you must bring me to him, Anna. I have a plan. Now that the first spell is broken, it follows that the other spells must be broken one after the other in a span of two days. The second spell has to be broken tonight."

"Why? What will happen if they're not broken in two days?"

"If we don't break the spells in two days, your mother, my parents, and the kingdom of Qwajo are doomed. They will forever be bound by the consequences of the spell. And now that Salas is on the loose, what do you think he'll do?"

"No! But. . . *we?* We will break the spell?"

"Yes. You and I, Anna."

"But. . . why me? And how? How can I possibly do that? I. . . I don't know any magic."

"You do," he clasps my hands tightly, urgently. "You just have to remember. I will make you remember, Anna. Will you let me help you?"

9

Anna

RE-LEARNING MAGIC

His deeply creased forehead bears the weight of the world. A world so foreign to me, but for some reason, so achingly familiar. Everything I've learned in the past hour is alien to me. And yet, I can't shake off the feeling of *déjà vu*.

Slowly, I nod. For the first time since we met, I smile at him. His face lights up, and I could swear his eyes have moistened, before he stands up and leads me to the side of the water.

"Good. We have eight hours to train. Then, tonight at midnight, you will go to the Castle."

***

He has been training me for the past ten hours, with only a few minutes of rest in between. But I can't complain.

He is a patient, knowledgeable teacher. He explains to me how magic works, shows me how, and then makes me do what I've learned until I get the hang of it.

Learning to use magic again is like fitting into beloved old clothes of my younger years. It's easy, comfortable, and liberating all at the same time.

I didn't know I had it in me, but now that I re-learned to use my magic, even I am amazed at the power I have at my fingertips.

It's fun manipulating objects, making them disappear and appear, possessing super strength and speed, and blasting away anything and anyone with a sonic beam.

It's a pity I can't fly, though. Not yet. Liam says some magic takes time to re-surface.

While Liam as a Tamawo takes his energy from the water, I, as a witch, get mine from the moon. But the magic which that energy powers up comes from within me—from all three elements: heart, mind, and body.

"You musn't be controlled only by your emotions, like anger," he states as we finish our training and prepare for an hour of shut-eye before we go to the castle. "Magic cast only by emotions is incomplete and may not have the result you desire."

"But I was able to get the phone off the ground this morning," I argue.

"And yet, it didn't stay in your hand, did it? It fell. You need to put your entire being into casting your magic."

"I understand."

He beams with pride. "You did great today. Your magic will slowly return to its former strength every time you use it."

I nod absent-mindedly, my eyes focused on the bed.

Are we sleeping in one bed? The thought scares me, but I can't ignore the thrill it also brings.

That embrace we shared earlier almost made me forget the gravity of our situation. I wanted to remain in his arms forever. Only the thought of my parents in the hands of that evil Warlock woke me up to reality.

But throughout the day, his physical proximity has unnerved me countless times. It has taken an almost superhuman effort on my part not to let him see that I'm affected by the nearness of him.

Every touch, every brush of his skin against mine, every time our eyes meet, – accidental or otherwise– is a powerful pull of something I cannot fully comprehend.

What is it about him that makes me both awed and excited by the mere thought of his touch?

"This bed is big enough for both of us, Anna," he teases. "I won't do anything you don't want to do, if that's what you're thinking."

I blush. "Don't read my mind."

"I didn't. It's written all over your face," he chuckles. "Besides, I can't read your mind, even if I wanted to. And you can't read mine, too."

Curious, I cock my head to one side. "Really? Why is that?"

He shrugs. "That's just how it is."

"Hmm. Have you told me everything? Because I feel like you're holding something back."

He purses his lips, and I can't help but be drawn to them. I hastily lower my eyes.

Not fast enough, though, because he grins adorably before he replies to me, "I've told you what you need to know. . . for now. It's better if some things come back naturally to you."

I want to say something more, but he gets into bed, putting a stop to our conversation. I follow suit. For some time, we lay on our backs, side by side, in comfortable silence.

Then he turns to me and asks, "You said your mother talked to you in your dream. I can only surmise that she used your subconscious as a portal where she could meet you and communicate with you. Have you had other dreams like that? Of other people? Like my parents? Or anyone else?"

I swallow hard. How can I tell him that except for that one dream, my dreams have always been of *him* and of *us making love?*

I shake my head. "No. It was only my mother."

"Now *you're* the one who's holding information from *me.*"

I gasp, turning to him, our faces dangerously close. "No, I'm not!"

"It's written all over your face again, Anna. Tell me, who did you dream about?"

I open my mouth to speak, but our eyes meet, and suddenly, everything stops.

It's like being thrown into a suspended animation where only he and I are the only ones that matter, and everything has evaporated into nothingness.

All I can see and feel is *him.* I can feel his emotions as if they are my own. I feel his longing. . . his regrets. . . his joy. . . his sadness. . . and the heat of his passion.

He licks his lips and dips his face toward mine.

"Anna. . . ," he murmurs, his breath hot and urgent.

Like it was in my dream.

My eyes widen, and I draw in a quick breath. In one fluid motion, I get up from the bed, muttering, "I. . . I think I'll have a glass of water."

I don't wait for an answer and stride to the kitchen. I gulp the water down and stay there for about ten minutes. When I come back to the bed, his back is turned.

Suddenly, I feel guilty for my seemingly violent reaction to the kiss that had been forthcoming.

"Liam, I'm sorry. . . please don't think that. . ."

He cuts me off mid-sentence. "Go to sleep, Anna. You'll need your strength."

I bite my lip. Beneath the veneer of his harsh tone, I feel him hurting.

And *it hurts that I've hurt him.*

Why am I feeling this way?

When I doze off, my dream is empty.

10

Anna

THE SECOND SPELL

ONE HOUR BEFORE MIDNIGHT, I AM PASSING THROUGH THE open Castle gates, coming from the drawbridge.

There are only two guards. I recognize them as the two men who tried to kill me. They follow me as I continue to walk forward, no doubt obeying Salas' instructions.

Up in the skies, the moon is at its fullest. I close my eyes, drinking in the energy from it, harnessing it for what lies beyond the Castle doors.

I press my hands on my stomach, feeling the bulge of the sculpture inside the kangaroo pocket covering the front of my sweatshirt. I inhale deeply, summoning all the courage that I need.

The tasks ahead seem insurmountable. If–*and that's a big if*–the second spell is broken tonight, there's still the third spell. Which, according to Liam, he has no memory of what it was or how to break it. To top it all, he doesn't remember the Source.

How frustrating. If only the Trifecta is here for the answers to my million questions.

The last day has been a roller coaster of events that can only happen in storybooks. Everything I believed to be the truth turned out to be fallacies created by magic.

Magic that I now possess and must use to try to break an unbreakable curse.

But I feel there is more that Liam hasn't told me. He's hiding something from me. Something that is truly relevant to all that's happening.

***

Yet there is no time for despair or weakness. I straighten my back, square my shoulders, and march inside the Castle, into the Great Hall. The two guards stay outside the doors.

Like the rest of Qwajo, the Hall is dark and gloomy. The main entrance is dirty and full of rubble. The high-beamed ceiling is thick with cobwebs. Roots and branches of dead vines encircle the rows of marble pillars. The windows are broken and dilapidated.

At the end of the large, long room, there is a gigantic painting which covers the entire expanse of the wall.

It's a hyperrealistic painting of the first king, King Leroy. The man who built a kingdom that is now a mere shadow of its greatness. His right hand is raised slightly, holding a dagger. His left hand is around his Queen, standing next to him. She is carrying their infant son, the then Crown Prince, who must have been barely a year old.

Below the painting, on a raised platform, an ivory throne is at the center, with two smaller thrones on each side of it.

I spot four people, and walk toward them. As I near them, my heart pounds with a mixture of joy and apprehension. I stop some ten feet away.

I see my mother smiling at me, albeit wanly. It's true! She is awake and seems to be well, but weak.

Beside her, the Queen is seated on the right throne, her beautiful face ashen and gaunt. She is wearing a long dress, but her emaciated arms are still glimpsed beneath the sheer fabric. For a moment, it strikes me that she resembles Liam, except for the eyes.

And then, sitting on the ivory throne, is the Duke, Lord George.

Or so I think.

Because while his body and arms are those of a man, his face and legs are those of a horse. So, this is the curse of the Omni.

Lord George has become a *tikbalang,* and he appears to be under a dazing spell. His horse head is drooped to his chest and he is immobile.

Mr. Salamanca–*Salas*–steps forward from the Duke's left side, his palms up as his voice echoes throughout the Hall.

"Stop right there, Anna! Where is the owl?"

"My mother first!" I yell back at him. "Let her walk toward me. When I have her, I will give you the owl!"

Salas' nostrils flare, but he signals my mother to walk toward me.

When she reaches me, I hug her tight, laughing and crying at the same time.

She speaks to me with a hoarse, weak voice. "I'm glad Liam has been freed. I trust he has told you what you need to know?"

"Yes, Mom. I. . . I don't fully understand everything that's happening, I'm just so glad you're okay now. But where's Dad?" I ask.

"Salas left him behind under a sleep spell. He's fine, Anna. And *you* will be fine. I trust you."

Then she pulls me for another hug, and whispers in my ear, hurriedly. "Salas' power is not yet fully regained, but he has taken my magic. I don't have access to it, I can't use it. But once the second spell is broken, it will be returned to me. Anna, you have to act quickly. Or else, he will kill you."

"I know, Mom. I know. Don't worry," I assure her with a confidence I'm not exactly feeling.

"That's enough!" Salas shouts, breaking our conversation. "Give me the owl now, Anna!"

Putting my mother aside to safety, I shout back at him, "You mean, *this owl?*"

***

I hurl the sculpture upward, in the air, having taken it out surreptitiously from my front pocket the moment my mother and I hugged.

Startled, Salas takes a step back, his eyes on the statue.

I take advantage of the moment and swiftly conjured saltwater from my right hand. As soon as the water touches the statue, Liam materializes, leaping onto Salas and knocking him down to the floor.

Before Salas can move, Liam binds his hands behind his back with a binding spell, incapacitating him. He stands him up and snarls at his face.

"It's over, Salas! I don't know how you got out of your prison, but you and your black magic are now finished!"

Instead of anger, Salas roars with laughter. "Don't be too sure, my Prince. I had help then, from someone you would not have expected. And I have help—*now!"*

Suddenly, a blood-curdling, high-pitched neigh blares in the air, followed by a woman's scream.

My mother and I turn to the source of the sounds. We both gasp out loud when we see the Queen being held by Lord George, his hands around her bony neck, which can snap at any moment.

Salas and the Duke have fooled us all. The Duke wasn't dazed. He has been waiting for this exact moment before making his move.

"Mother!" Liam cries out.

Salas leers at him. "Release me, or the Queen is dead. You wouldn't want that on your conscience, my Prince. Would you?"

Liam grits his teeth, his face red with rage. But he knows he has no choice. He unbinds Salas with one flick of his hand.

As soon as Salas' hands are released, he strikes Liam with a killing blast, hitting him squarely on the chest.

***

Blood spurts out of Liam as he stumbles backward before falling down on the floor with a resounding thud.

"No! Liam!" I scream.

Furious, I attack Salas with my left hand and, with my right hand, the Duke. My magic flings them up to the high ceiling and paralyzes them, and I leave them hanging there.

I run to Liam, my heart pounding.

My mother goes to help the Queen, who is whimpering, "My son, my son!"

Crying, I cradle Liam's head on my lap, my hands on his chest, trying to stop the bleeding.

His beautiful face is pained and his eyes are turning gray. He is at death's doors. He coughs, and his white teeth are stained with red. He touches my face with his hand.

"Anna. . . my Anna. . . I'm sorry. . . this isn't what I planned," he mutters.

"Stop talking and let me heal you," I admonish him, my voice trembling. "There must be a spell to heal you. There must be!"

My mother and the Queen come up silently behind me.

"Mom, please teach me how to heal him. Please! Please!" I beg her.

"That was a killing spell, Anna," Mom shakes her head slowly. "There's no spell to counter it."

"No! No. . ." I whimper.

The Queen's face is covered with tears. "This isn't what's supposed to happen. The Power of Three spell was meant to protect us. . . "

Hearing her last words, my eyes widen as realization dawns on me.

"That's it! That's it! The second spell! If the second spell is broken, he would be healed! Because the Power of Three spell overpowers every spell! Isn't that right?"

My mother and the Queen exchanged looks before Mom says, "Yes, that's right. You're right, Anna!"

"Then what is it? How do we break it?" I plead to the Queen. "Tell me, please, your Majesty!"

"Oh, dear child," the Queen replies to me, "Liam is the bearer and breaker of the second spell. Only he can do it."

I turn back to Liam and gently shake him. "Liam, what's the second spell? How do you break it? Let me help you!"

"I . . . can't . . . tell you," he whispers. His voice is dangerously low and slow.

"Why won't you tell me?" I cry. "What good would that do if you're dead? I don't want you to die, Liam!"

"I can. . . tell you, though. . . ," he continues, catching his breath, seemingly not hearing what I just said, "that

I've loved you . . . even before I laid eyes on you. And . . . I will love you . . . till eternity."

Sobbing, I break down as I rest my forehead against his. "Please don't die! Liam. . . Liam, you were right. I lied when you asked me if I dreamed of someone else aside from my mother. It was you, Liam! You were in my dreams. . . and I don't know why, or how, but. . . you are in my heart, too. I love you!"

"I know. . . ," he smiles weakly. "You. . . just have to. . . remember."

Our faces are too close to each other. His lips are slightly open, and the pull of their allure is unbearable.

"Anna. . . you're mine. . . and I am yours," he mutters, before lifting his head to meet my waiting lips.

We kiss.

I feel both of us being lifted from the ground, and we swirl and we twirl, but I am not frightened, nor am I dizzy. I hear thunder and rain, and feel the gentle warmth of the sun, all at the same time.

And then in a flash, *I remember:* him and me and Elro as toddlers, playing and laughing together; Liam and I as teenagers, sharing our first dance and our first kiss; Liam, kneeling before me as he proposed to me; Liam and I on our wedding day, with the rest of the kingdom partying and rejoicing with us; Liam and I, alone at last on our wedding night, making love over and over again, not getting enough of each other.

I open my eyes to find him smiling at me, both of us standing. His wound is gone, and my mother and the Queen are both teary-eyed but happy, watching us.

I was the second spell, and Liam has freed me at last.

11

Liam

THE CALM BEFORE THE STORM

As soon as my lips touch hers, the spell is broken.

Mother said my kiss would break the spell which erased Anna's memory. But it shouldn't be just a kiss. It should be reciprocated with the same emotion I am feeling.

Love.

I've known in my heart that it was me she was dreaming about.

I made sure of it.

From the confines of the owl sculpture where I had been hidden, I talked to her every single day. I whispered to her how I longed to see her again. . . talk to her again. . . touch her again. . . make love to her again.

Her dreams were not just dreams.

They were memories of me.

They were memories of us.

They were memories of the passionate love we shared.

***

Simultaneous with the breaking of the second spell, my mother and Anna's mother, Mona, regain their magical powers. The Queen's health and Mona's strength are also restored.

But it also means that a fragment of the curse inflicted on the Duke is lifted—and Anna's magic on them as well.

Salas and the Duke drop from the ceiling. Quickly, Salas prevents their fall with his magic, and they float safely down to the floor.

Before they could take one step, my mother and Mona hit them with successive blasts of lightning bolts.

Salas is quicker, though. Palms up, he conjures a force field and encloses them both in it, protecting them from the blasts, before they proceed to fly out of the Hall, almost knocking us down on their way.

I catch a glimpse of Uncle George's familiar face, but he still has horse legs, hooves, and a tail.

"They're escaping!" Mona shouts. "Don't let them escape!"

Anna and I raise our hands at the same time, throwing both sonic and light energy at the fugitives. The powerful combination of energy hits the force field and tears it, but Salas swiftly flies away before it is completely destroyed.

We all watch helplessly as Salas and Uncle George vanish into the skies.

"They'll be back," my mother says. "We must be prepared."

Mona nods, her jaw set. She's always been brave, like my Anna. "I'll fortify the Castle with a protection spell. Anna can help me."

"No, Mona," the Queen firmly disagrees with her best friend. "*I* will help you. Let's give the children some time for themselves."

Anna's face turns red, and I smile as I grasp her hand.

The Queen is not known for tactfulness, but I love my mother. She is a strong woman, but she is also compassionate and understanding. She knows how much I've missed my wife.

Mona's eyes twinkle as she smiles at us. "Of course, your Majesty. As always, you are right. Although the rest of the kingdom is still under the curse, the Castle is slowly returning to normal. They should go up to their residence to rest."

***

All around us, the effects of the second spell are wearing off. The Hall is changing from dark and dirty to bright and stark white, replete with lights, modern fixtures, and furniture. The glass windows are whole again, and the dead vines which covered the pillars are gone, replaced with precious stones of different colors and sizes.

A group of ladies in waiting appear at the entrance, freed from the spell that turned them into rubble. Troops of guards rush in, no doubt also released from the spell, encircling the Queen, ready to heed her command. Another group of guards has apprehended the two men who tried to kill Anna.

And on the west side of the Hall, a grand staircase is sprouting out, leading to the adjacent building housing our vast residences.

It is a magnificent sight to behold, to see once more the grandeur of the Castle of Qwajo.

Anna smiles and curtsies before the Queen, showing her respect and gratitude. "Thank you, my Queen, for your kindness."

"But, Mother," I ask, suddenly remembering, "what about Father? What about the King?"

At the mention of my father, my mother's face becomes gloomy again. "I can't feel him here, my son. He's not anywhere in the Castle. But I know he's alive. He might be in limbo. Let us worry about the third spell first. Once the third spell is broken, your father will appear. I'm sure of it."

Mona agrees. "That's right. Isn't that so, Anna?"

We all turn to Anna, who returns our gaze, perplexed.

"Me?" Her forehead is creased with confusion. "Why me?"

Mona and the Queen exchange looks.

"You don't remember?" Mona blurts out.

My mother's face crumples. "Oh, dear child, I thought with the breaking of the second spell. . ."

Anna clutches my arm. "Liam?"

I swallow hard. "I still don't know the third spell, Anna. Only *you* know what the third spell is. And you alone knows *how to break* it."

12

Anna

THE HAPPY DREAM

We're sitting side by side on the gigantic bed in our room. I remember this room so vividly.

It was me who decorated this place before our wedding. Liam gave me a free hand in everything—except the bed.

He was the one who chose the sturdy, four-poster bed frame and its soft, thick mattress.

It's nice to be back home. The opulent interior doesn't give me comfort, though. I sigh heavily.

Liam puts his arms around me, cuddling me. "Don't worry. It'll come back to you, babe."

His familiar term of endearment makes my heart flutter. We've always been 'babe' to each other. How could I have ever forgotten that?

Yet the reality of the situation doesn't make me feel completely at ease.

"But when? We need to break the third spell in twelve hours. And I'm sure, right now, Salas and the Duke are plotting how to break the protection spell around the Castle."

"True," he muses, "but let's not cross the bridge until we get there, shall we? I'm just really thankful right now that we're back on our bed together." He grins. "I missed this bed! I really love this bed, you know?"

I know he's trying to lighten me up, so I play along. "Of course you do. You picked this one out of the many beds the woodsmith showed you. Good thing you did, because he nearly went out of his mind trying to please you."

He snuggles closer, chuckling. "And I gave him a huge reward for his efforts, remember?" Then he turns serious. "But it's not the bed I really missed."

I give him an impish smile. "I know. I missed you too, babe."

"How can you miss me when you didn't remember who I was? You thought I was fat and ugly!" he teases.

"Well, now that I remember everything, I realize I missed you, silly," I joke back.

We share a laugh.

We've always had easy, funny conversations. It's one of the things I love about him.

Afterward, I cup his face with my hands and get serious.

"I really missed you, too."

"I missed you more."

"You did?"

"Yes," he whispers, his lips almost touching mine, his burning desire evident. "Let me show you how much."

And all through the night he did.

We did not waste a second as we familiarized ourselves with each other's body, explored one another again, pleasured each other, until we both reached the peak together—more times than I can count.

***

I'm dreaming again. This time, though, it's a happy dream.

Liam and I are strolling hand in hand in the Castle's vast garden, filled with abundant greenery and all kinds of flowers.

I am telling him a funny story.

He laughs. The beautiful sound of his laughter fills the garden.

But then, I hear another laughter.

It's high-pitched. It's contagious.

It's more beautiful than Liam's.

It's from another person.

And like Liam's, it sounds familiar to me.

I start to turn around to see who it is.

Before I can find out, an ear-shattering, terrifying howl is heard—the howl of a wild, humongous animal.

A strong earthquake shakes the garden, and everything trembles violently.

I lose my balance and fall to the ground.

Then, the light disappears, and everywhere becomes dark.

Pitch-black dark.

13

Liam

THE WHITE BAKUNAWA

"Anna! Anna!" I was awakened by the ear-shattering noise and the violent shaking of the bed. The earthquake was so strong that I got thrown off the bed and straight to the wall. It knocked my breath out.

When I came around, I see only darkness around me.

Anna is nowhere.

I flick my fingers, and bright, white light shines from my right palm. I can't find Anna.

It's too dark. I flick my left palm to add more light.

I still don't find Anna anywhere.

I turn my palms forward. Horrified, I see the deep, wide crater before me. A few more inches, and I would have been plunged down there!

Despite the utter darkness, I manage to illuminate some areas. I inspect my surroundings, and the hairs on my arms stand at the devastation I see around us.

The building where we were is split into two, and a very wide crater now stands in between.

Curious, I inspect the crater. It's deep—too deep. I see water below.

It looks like *something colossal* came from under the water, burrowed into the earth, and burst itself out into the surface.

I hear my name, but the voice sounds too low and far away.

Frowning, I search for the voice. I turn my palms farther, to the other side of the crater. I gasp out loud as I see Anna there, sitting on what was left of our bed.

"Anna! Babe, are you okay?"

She shakes her head. She looks weak—too weak.

I concentrate, trying to transport myself to her location. But the crater is too wide, and for some reason, my magic is blocked.

I can't go to her. I grind my teeth helplessly.

"Anna, babe. Wait for me, I'll find a way!" I yell.

She nods. Then she mouths, raises her hand, and points a finger upward.

My palms follow where she is pointing, and I am shocked at what I see.

A humongous white beast is floating in the dark skies!

A *bakunawa*. A giant serpent-like dragon. Its body is long and sinuous, coiling and twisting like a snake as it moves. White, silvery scales cover its sleek body. Its head is crowned with horns, and fangs as long as daggers line its mouth. Its gigantic wings are flapping wildly, almost covering the skies.

That's why my magic is not working. Its wings are driving off my energy.

This white *bakunawa* caused this massive devastation.

But that's not all. Because I realize now why it is too dark.

The bakunawa has swallowed the moon.

Its belly is engorged, the shape of the moon visible.

That's why Anna is weak.

The moon is gone.

The source of her energy is gone.

***

I thrust my palms farther upward, zeroing in on the *bakunawa*. My eyes widen when I see Salas and Uncle George sitting on its head, clearly controlling the beast.

Salas said he was able to escape from prison with help. So this is the help he mentioned. The *bakunawa* helped him escape, and it is helping them now.

Hastily, I drop my palms, and the stark darkness of the skies returns.

But the light from my palms has already been noticed by the *bakunawa* and its riders. I hear Salas scream, "Kill them! Kill those two!"

With a tremendous roar, the *bakunawa* swoops down toward us, its mouth ablaze with red fire, ready to spit hot flames that will devour us.

I stare destitutely at Anna, whose face is streaked with tears.

The shadow of the *bakunawa's* wings envelops us in darkness.

I squeeze my eyes shut.

14

Liam

CORNERED

WHEN I OPEN MY EYES AGAIN, I FIND MYSELF STILL ALIVE. I breathe in sharply. I am back at the Great Hall, on the raised platform where the thrones are. The floor is lit with somber and gloomy light, cast by magic.

Beside me, Anna is seated on the floor with Mona, who is also feeling weak.

My mother's face comes into my view. "My son, I'm glad I got you out of there on time."

"Mother! Thank you for saving us." We embrace warmly as Mona and Anna look on.

If not for my mother's quick reflexes, we would have been toast moments ago.

But from far above, we hear the beast's roar, and the air becomes heated. It's swooping down on us—and fast.

Our eyes meet with trepidation.

Quickly, my mother releases me and stands up. She raises her arms, wielding her magic. She sets up an invisible shield around us, encompassing the platform, the ceiling above it, and the wall with the painting behind us.

With Mona and Anna's magic gone with the moon, I help my mother, fortifying the shield with my own power.

Just in time too, because the *bakunawa* hits it with a strong burst of flame. Its force makes us stagger backward.

"This *bakunawa's* strength is unbelievable!" I exclaim, catching my breath.

Mona agrees, her voice pained and low. "It can only come from black magic, which Salas is using to control it."

Salas and Uncle George are alighting from the back of the beast and landing on the floor.

Uncle George is a grotesque sight, having the face, body, and arms of a man, but the hooves, legs, and tail of a horse. The curse upon him has not been fully broken. He's *half-tikbalang,* half-human.

Salas' deep-set eyes are glowing red, his powers gaining strength from the dark magic released from the breaking of the second spell. He raises his palms, adding magical force to the *bakunawa's* attacks on us.

The shield is resisting, but I can feel its magic diminishing.

Any time now, it will rip open.

"Mother, we cannot hold off Salas and his beast for long," I grunt, boosting my strength as much as I can. "We need Father! Where could he be?"

"I sense his presence, my son," the Queen reveals, her jaw tense with the effort she's exerting. "He's here! He's around here somewhere! But we still can't see him. I fear he can't get out of the limbo he's in. Anna must remember the third spell—and *quick!*"

Without breaking my magic's hold on the shield, I turn to Anna with a questioning look.

She shakes her head, slowly and painfully. I bite my lip, trying to suppress the panic in my throat.

If the third spell is not broken in time, we're all dead, and the Source will fall into the hands of Uncle George.

Just then, the *bakunawa's* fire and Salas' magic release a particularly powerful blast. It is so strong that all of us are catapulted forcefully backward.

We are slammed against the wall behind us with a loud thud.

The impact makes me lose my grip on my magic, and for a second, my vision becomes blurry. I shake my head to regain my wits and look around, checking on the others.

I see my mother is still standing and holding off the subsequent attacks—but just barely.

Mona is pointing a trembling finger behind me, mouthing, "The shield. . . there's a small tear there. . ."

And Anna. . . Anna is screaming, calling my name.

"Liam! Liam! I know what the third spell is! I know what it is!"

15

Anna

I REMEMBER IT NOW

"Liam! Liam! I know what the third spell is! I know what it is!"

My mother breathes in sharply. The Queen turns to me for a moment to smile, nodding in satisfaction. "Very good, Anna. Very good. You remember it now."

Yes. I remember it now.

I remember the chanting of the Trifecta in my mind, their solemn voices going round and round inside my head:

> "Source of Light
> Hide from sight.
> Till blood of blood
> Is spilled for love."

How could I have ever forgotten? What kind of person am I?

"Anna?" Liam shakes my shoulders, his face anxious. "What is it? What is the third spell?"

Before I can answer, another powerful blast hits the shield. We all watch in horror as it shatters like glass.

The Queen falls to the floor, screaming.

"Sonya!" My mother immediately goes to her.

Liam steps in front of me, his arms spread, *shielding me* from the explosion of magical dust.

I step backward, my back against the wall, my arms stretched out behind me.

Shielding the Source.

With a low, rolling growl, the *bakunawa* steps closer to us. The Queen tries to hit it with a sonic wave, but Salas is quick to bind her hands with a magic cord, while my mother can only watch.

Salas shouts, "Kill those two, Beast! I have no use for them!"

The *bakunawa* obeys, stepping closer to us—its belly bulging with the moon he had swallowed—until it's almost nose to nose with Liam. Then, its throat rumbles horrifically, readying the deadly flame to breathe out and obliterate us all.

But Liam exhales softly, his eyes fixated on the face of the beast.

"Father? Father, is that you?"

***

At those words, the beast abruptly stills, its nostrils flaring. The Queen and my mother gasp out loud.

Struck dumb by Liam's words, I take a peek from behind Liam's shoulder to stare at the beast's face, just inches away from us.

The beast's large, black, bloodshot eyes stare back at me. In this close proximity, I see a reddish map-like patch of skin on the middle of its forehead.

In all of Qwajo, *only King Treo has that distinctive birthmark.*

"Salas! Don't just stand there!" Uncle George commands. "Do something!"

Salas raises his right fist in the air and shakes it hard. He shouts, "Don't listen to him, Beast! Kill him! Kill him! I command you!"

The beast's eyes turn white. It lifts its head and shudders violently, evidently in extreme pain, resisting whatever is possessing it. Its wings thrash around, destroying everything in their path.

We cover our heads to protect ourselves from the falling debris.

Salas' voice rises above the noise of the havoc. "Kill, Beast! Kill!" He strikes the bakunawa's head with a blast of black light.

The beast's eyes return to their blackness. It growls loudly, and resumes its stance against us. It opens its mouth to deliver the molten fire to roast us.

***

Suddenly, the Queen's shrill scream penetrates the air. "No! No!"

Before anyone can move, my mother-in-law steps in between the bakunawa and Liam. Both Salas and the beast stop, and we all look on with bated breath at the scene before us.

She grasps the beast's face with both her hands, tears flowing down her cheeks. "It's you! *It's really you!* Oh, Treo, my love! What happened to you? What did they do to you?!"

The Duke roars in manic laughter. "Ah, my darling cousin! Blame it on the Trifecta's third spell, combined with Salas' last dark spell! The Omni Curse backfired on him, and Salas controls him now! I dare say Salas deserved this after what you've done to him!"

I cup my hand over my mouth. What is the Duke talking about? *What did the Queen do to Salas?*

Liam voices out my thoughts and asks Salas, "What did my mother do to you to deserve this? My grandfather took you under his wing and taught you everything! You were like a son to him!"

"And I wanted to be his son in every sense of the word!" Salas snarls. "I've loved your mother since we were children! But no, she rejected me and fell in love with a Tamawo!"

I cannot believe what I'm hearing. Salas turned evil all because of his unrequited love?

"You cannot take that against her!" My mother cries, her anger giving her strength. "You cannot take that against the kingdom that took you in when you were found washed ashore as a child! You're an ingrate! You and the Duke are the same!"

"Silence, you despicable witch!" The Duke bellows, throwing a paralyzing spell at my mother. He would have done it to the Queen, too, but Salas stopped him.

"Now, George, you don't need to lift a finger. I can do all these myself."

The Duke clicks his tongue. "You're always soft when it comes to my cousin, Salas," he drawls. "Better finish it now, or I will! Kill them all!"

***

But the Queen is oblivious to everything that's happening. Her attention is focused on the *bakunawa*. She continues to speak to the beast in a soft, sweet voice, stroking its rough, uneven cheeks.

"Please, my love, resist him. You are much stronger than his magic. You can resist Salas. I believe in you."

Her voice is proving to be like a siren song. The *bakunawa's* wild eyes turn soft. A big drop of tear falls to the Queen's left hand.

And still, she continues to plead with the monster. "Please, Treo, my love. Do it for me, my darling. Do it for us. Do it. . . for *your grandson!*"

16

Liam

THE THIRD SPELL

"*Grandson?*" My eyes bulge in shock. *I have a son?*

And then, it clicks.

I do! I do have a son! And his name is. . .

". . . Arion," Anna whispers from behind.

Slowly, I turn to face her. She is smiling with tears running down her cheeks. "Our son's name is Arion, babe."

With a groan, I grab her and embrace her tight.

My eyes water, as I finally remember: *the third spell is cast on our two-year-old son to protect him—the Source of Qwajo's magic.*

I still don't know where he is, or how to break the third spell. But the knowledge of having a son brings me so much happiness. My joy knows no bounds.

But it is short-lived.

***

Salas unleashes a black magical whip and wallops the back of the beast with it. The *bakunawa* roars horribly in pain. Its giant tail swivels violently, almost hitting Uncle George and Salas.

Enraged, Salas loops the whip around the beast's neck and pulls it back—hard. The Queen is thrown backward, and I hastily grab her to safety.

The *bakunawa* lets out a lengthy, ear-splitting bellow of pain. The harrowing sound echoes throughout the Castle, exits through the windows, and into the open air.

I am sure it's heard by the entire island.

"You. . . don't get. . . to disobey me, Tamawo!" Salas yells, straining to maintain his grip on the whip. He commands, "I control you! Kill. . . them . . . all!"

With a terrible last wail, the beast drops its head, and opens its enormous mouth, letting out a burst of deadly flames.

Without thinking, I raise my arms, blocking the fire with my meager magic. Swiftly, my mother helps out, adding power to my own. Mona and Anna look on helplessly.

But the *bakunawa's* scorching furnace is slowly breaking down our magic. I can feel its searing heat starting to penetrate. I know Mother can feel it, too.

I turn to her.

She has never looked more beautiful. . . and more sad.

And her eyes, streaming with tears, are gazing forward—at the beast—*at my father*—tenderly. . . lovingly. . . despite our impending death in his hands.

"It's okay. . . I forgive you, my darling," she whispers softly through trembling lips. "I will love you. . . always and forever."

***

Suddenly, the loud, blaring sound of a trumpet pierces the air. It is followed by heavy footsteps and a cacophony of resounding, deafening noise.

All of us—even Salas, Uncle George, and the beast—divert our attention toward the Hall's entrance.

At once, I breathe a sigh of relief as I realize where the noise is coming from.

A huge batallion of Tamawo, led by Elro blowing a trumpet, is marching forward. Their feet are stomping heavy and hard on the floor. They have neither swords nor guns for weapons. Instead, they carry steel pots and pans, which they are banging with great force along with their thunderous, unified shouts.

"Free the moon! Free the King! Free Qwajo!"

"The Tamawos!" Anna cries. "They're here!"

Mona nods. "The breaking of the second spell must have freed them from the non-intervention consequence of the Curse. And now, they're trying to make the *bakunawa* spit out the moon."

"Yes," my mother agrees. "The noise will scare the beast to spit it out. Be ready, Mona! Once the moon is expelled, your powers will be back! You too, Anna!"

Mona nods. Anna doesn't speak, but I notice that she slowly steps backward until her back is against the wall where the painting is.

My brows arch. I've never known her to back away from a fight. Why is she doing it now, of all times?

Before I can ask her, the noise becomes louder and louder, hurting our ears as the batallion nears.

The *bakunawa's* eyes bulge in terror, its stomach grumbling vigorously.

"No! No!" Salas screams as Uncle George cowardly ducks behind a pillar.

Salas tries to stop the noises, but my mother intercepts his magic at once. He curses, knowing he is unable to exert more effort with his hands full of two simultaneous powerful spells—controlling the beast's mind and the magical whip.

With a pulsating, screeching howl, the *bakunawa* ejects the moon.

There is a burst of bright, white light as it illuminates the whole Hall for a few moments, blinding us all.

17

Anna

THE SACRIFICE

WHEN THE QUEEN TELLS US TO PREPARE, MY MIND WORKS quickly. I slowly step backward, my hands groping the wall.

Liam throws me a questioning look before he crouches, his hands over his ears as the noises increase tenfold.

With a pulsating, screeching howl, the *bakunawa* ejects the moon.

The bright, white light burst out of the moon, filling the entire hall with its luminescence, blinding everyone—except me and my mother.

The whole time the moon is blinding everyone, we are soaking up its energy, filling ourselves with it.

After a few seconds, when I have my fill, I grab Liam's arm and yank him to me.

"Do you trust me?" I ask him, hurriedly.

He opens his eyes for a bit, and for an instant, he looks at me in confusion. Then he replies, "Yes. Yes, of course, I trust you!"

I smile and raise my hand, summoning the dagger from the painting behind us.

It flies obediently to me, its hilt landing snugly on my palm.

I grasp it tight.

Then in one swift move, *I thrust its blade into Liam's heart—once*—before I pull it out and stand back.

His eyes widen in disbelief before he closes them as he falls to the floor.

Amid the blinding light, the noises, and the roar of the beast, my love lays dead before me.

***

But there is no time to grieve.

I straighten up my spine, and scream at the top of my lungs in the middle of the commotion.

"Mom! My Queen!"

They turn to me and see Liam at my feet. Their eyes harden, knowing what comes next.

"It's time!" I bellow.

They nod in unison, their mouths set in determination.

I breathe in sharply. . . before I stab myself in the chest with the dagger.

I fall—beside my husband, my love—before my eyes close, welcoming death.

18

Mona

NO TIME TO LOSE

THERE IS NO TIME TO LOSE.

The moon's light is diminishing. It is slowly ascending, floating upward to the skies, where it rightfully belongs.

The noise is dying down. The Tamawos are still here, but they know they have played their part. They are merely watching, waiting for the breaking of the third spell—and subsequently, the lifting of the Omni Curse.

The *bakunawa* is starting to pull itself together, and will surely fly away to escape.

And Salas and the Duke will wield their black magic again when they get the chance.

I take the dagger smoothly from my daughter's chest with my right hand. With my left hand, I grab hold of Sonya's hand.

"Ready?" I ask my best friend.

"Ready as ever," she grimly replies.

My Queen, my best friend since childhood, continues to inspire awe in me even now. Her gentle, ethereal beauty masks an extraordinary strength of character that is tempered and composed—a disciplined iron will that many, including George and Salas, underestimate.

I was the wild one. *I* was the one who needed to be tamed, to be taught how to control my fear, my hardheadedness, my magic.

I'm glad Sonya had the patience to mentor me when I needed it the most. She taught me how to have a firm hand and a focused mind. It proved to be useful when I was able to communicate with my daughter, breaking through the Zone.

And today of all days, I must use those skills to the fullest.

Sonya releases a magic leash toward the *bakunawa*. It wraps itself around the beast's neck, she pulls it, and shouts, "NOW, MONA, NOW!"

With a shrill scream, I impale the dagger—dripping with the blood of Liam and Anna—deep to the hilt on the painting on the wall.

18

Queen Sonya

THE LIFTING OF THE CURSE

As the dagger is buried to the hilt in the painting, the wall starts to crack open. I grit my teeth, alert and waiting.

This is the tricky part.

Once the third spell is broken, we have to act fast. If we're even one second late, Salas will be able to turn the tide against us. George will get hold of the Source, and Qwajo will have a new, evil king.

We will all be doomed.

Not if I can help it.

I fix my eyes on the crack as lightning strikes in all directions, and thunder claps everywhere.

I'm holding my breath. My heart is pounding against my ribs.

This is the moment of truth.

At the other end of the magic strand, the bakunawa—*Treo*—is wiggling, trying to escape.

That can't happen.

All three members of the Trifecta must be present when the Curse is lifted.

If Treo escapes, if I lose hold of him, the breaking of the third spell will be incomplete, and all of us will die.

I stare at the bodies of my son and my daughter-in-law lying at our feet.

If we die, Liam and Anna's deaths will be futile.

Please, please, please, my grandson. Come out now. Before it's too late.

***

As if he heard me, Arion suddenly bursts out from the hole in the wall, running straight into Mona, giggling, "Grandma! Grandma!"

Arion is glowing brightly, suffused with the Light.

The Hall shakes and trembles.

Mona hurriedly grasps Arion's hand. Instantly, the Light covers her hand and her entire body, creeps into mine, and travels to the magic strand, covering the *bakunawa* as well.

All four of us are now glowing with the Light.

In the blink of an eye, the beast turns back into Treo, his hand gripping the strand at once to maintain his connection with me.

My Tamawo husband, with his flowing white hair and pale skin, is back. He is smiling as he flies, landing beside me. Then his face becomes grim, and I know he remembers how he almost killed me.

I shake my head once, indicating that all should be forgotten and that we still have work to do.

He nods. Hand in hand, all four of us—me, Treo, Mona, and Arion—glowing bright with the Light, turn to face and confront Salas.

He is standing a few feet from us, having gathered his wits after all the commotion.

The lifting of the Curse has given him back his full powers, and he is just about to use them against us.

But this time, we are faster.

Faster, wiser, and stronger.

Before he can wield his magic, we strike at him with full force. His fingers break, one by one. He screams in pain.

But it seems his black heart is incapable of remorse. He chides, "Is that what you got? Child's play! I am more powerful than you all . . ."

Before he can finish his sentence, we raise all our hands. His eyes turn white.

He howls, "What. . . what did you do? Bring me back my sight! Bring me back my eyes! I will kill you all! I will kill you!"

Treo sighs. "Enough, my Queen. He will not repent, though you want him to. And Arion should not witness such evil at his young age."

I understand. I nod.

Unlike Salas, we are merciful. We do not prolong agony.

We twist our entwined hands once. Salas disintegrates into dust, along with his black magic.

We were wrong when we tried to defeat Salas and protect Arion by hiding him using the Omni Curse.

Because all along, Arion was the missing key to ultimately vanquishing black magic.

Behind us, we hear George's voice. He has also returned to his former self, the remaining hooves and tail of a *tikbalang* now gone.

"Cousin! Sonya, I am sorry for trying to usurp the throne!" He pleads. "I was wrong! Please, let's start over again. I will obey you! I am your servant for life! I'll do anything you want me to!"

But Mona flings a spell on George. It penetrates the pillar from where George is hiding, hitting him head on. My cousin, the usurper of the throne, becomes a toad.

With a long, high-pitched croak, it jumps frantically in circles, before going out of the Hall.

Treo and I stare, open-mouthed at Mona. She curtsies and smiles apologetically. "Forgive me, my Queen. But he doesn't deserve to be human. Let him repent as a toad."

For the first time in a long time, I laugh heartily. My best friend has always made me crack with laughter, and I love her for it.

Mona chuckles, Treo joins in, and Arion—*Arion! my darling grandson*—begins to giggle, too.

He thinks we're playing the dungeons and dragons game his grandfather has taught him, like we used to. He doesn't really know what's going on, being only two years old.

Mona gives him a kiss.

Treo pulls me into a warm, tight embrace.

It is finished. The kingdom is safe.

Liam and Anna's sacrifices have not been in vain.

20

King Treo

SWEET REVENGE

I WRAP MY ARMS TIGHT AROUND MY WIFE, MY QUEEN— never wanting to let go of her warm body against mine, fusing the beating of my heart to hers.

As a Tamawo, I could have had all the women available at my disposal. It's easy for us. Women tend to gravitate toward our good looks and well-toned physique, especially when we make use of our mystical saliva to entice women into our bed and make them fall in love with us.

That's what Salas mistakenly thought.

He thought I used magic on Sonya. He thought I enchanted her to choose me and make her fall in love with me instead of him.

He didn't realize it was the other way around.

Sonya enchanted *me*—with her beauteous face, her quiet strength, her quick wit, and her kind soul. I fell for her hard and fast.

I voluntarily gave up my immortality for a lifetime with her, and I will never ever regret doing that.

***

Salas never accepted Sonya's refusal of him. He never accepted that Sonya only saw him as her adopted brother.

It fueled his hatred toward me.

I sensed it long ago, even before Sonya and I were married. I thought his antipathy would go away as time passed.

It didn't. It turned out that he had been plotting revenge ever since.

When he teamed up with George against us, and we were forced to use the Power of Three spell to overpower his dark magic, I didn't realize he had unknowingly taken a strand of my white hair during the battle.

As we finished chanting the third spell, he tried to use my hair to counter it.

He couldn't, but it caused the spell to rebound on us—especially me.

I was shocked to find myself in the body of a *bakunawa* and extremely disgusted to have to obey Salas' commands. But I wasn't able to do anything about it.

Salas had his sweet revenge. Not only did he turn me into the very opposite of beauty that we Tamawos are known for, he was also able to humiliate me in the most demeaning way possible.

Above all, he almost made me kill my wife.

I shudder as I remember that I almost killed the love of my life. I know Sonya understands that it wasn't intentional, that I was controlled by Salas' dark magic, and that everything ended well for Qwajo.

That Liam and Anna's sacrifices have not been in vain.

Even so, I can't—*won't*—forgive myself for what I did.

I squeeze my eyes tight as I make a silent vow: *I will spend every waking moment of my life making it up to my wife.*

I will make it my life's mission to make Sonya happy.

That will be my sweet revenge on Salas.

Epilogue

Anna

I'M IN THE ZONE AGAIN.

I'm with my beautiful man. His name is Liam.

He's the Crown Prince of the enchanted kingdom of Qwajo. He's also a Prince in Kisignan, the Tamawo realm.

He's my husband, my other half, the one I vowed to spend the rest of my life with.

And I plan to do just that.

***

When the third spell was broken, the Omni Curse was also lifted.

It brought us back from death and reunited us with our family.

The kingdom of Qwajo has been delivered from its enemy. Salas, the Warlock, is vanquished.

Qwajo's wealth and prosperity, including trade between our kingdom, the mainland, and the world, have resumed.

The citizens are back to normal, though they don't remember anything. It's just as well. They are spared the horrors of what happened to their beloved monarchy.

My father and my mother resumed their duties at the Castle. Dad is the Steward responsible for all financial and legal matters concerning the castle's estates. He was furious when he learned he was turned into a pawnshop owner, but after some time, he learned to laugh about it.

My mother, of course, is the Queen's personal assistant and protector.

The King and Queen traveled all over Qwajo and saw to it that everything and everyone were back to the way they were before. They also visited Kisigna, where they profusely thanked the Tamawos for their help and rewarded them with gold.

All portals between Qwajo and Kisigna were re-opened, and every Tamawo can again freely interact with Qwajonians, as it has always been.

Most of all, the Source of Qwajo's magic, Arion—our son—is safe from the evil designs of Duke George, who is now a wandering toad.

***

The Trifecta has been wrong in assuming that they can defeat black magic by themselves alone. As powerful as they are, they do not possess the purity and innocence of the Source.

For what can defeat darkness, if not with Light?

King Leroy was not only a powerful sorcerer but also a wise one. He knew the future of Qwajo belonged to the young, and so he entrusted the Source of magic—the Light—to his infant son.

It has always been that way, ever since.

Every first offspring becomes the gatekeeper to the most powerful magic in all of Qwajo.

And Arion, being half-sorcerer, half-Tamawo, and half-witch, has inherited a power beyond anyone's expectation, more powerful than the Trifecta and us, his parents, combined.

All of us have made a solemn vow to train him and make sure that that power will be harnessed to its full potential for the greater good of Qwajo and mankind as a whole.

***

"I know you're still awake," Liam's deep, warm voice breaks my thoughts. He has just come in after putting Arion to sleep, an evening ritual between father and son.

He lies beside me, and traces his finger from my hairline down to the tip of my nose and further, to my lips, lingering there.

"Mmm. . . ," I smile. "I'm just relishing the feel of our bed once again."

"Ah, yes. The woodsmith truly deserved the reward I gave him after he'd made the exact replica of our old bed."

"I still think you should have given him a yacht," I joke.

He grins and taps my nose softly. "He wanted the helicopter, babe. It's his choice."

His tone turns serious, though. "But. . . just the bed? You're relishing the feel of *just* our bed?"

"Of course not," I quip. "I'm also relishing our old-new room and house. Mom did a good job restoring our home, don't you think?"

"Seriously," he drawls, his voice petulant like a child's. "Those are what you're relishing?"

I laugh out loud. I do so love to tease my husband.

He is a Tamawo, the most beautiful species on earth, but his eyes and his heart are mine alone.

Every day with him is full of laughter and cherished moments. And every night. . . every night is filled with sweet, hot passion.

In one swift move, I climb on top of him. "What do you want to hear, babe?"

This time, I am the one doing the tracing. I trace my finger on his nose, to his lips, to his chin, and down to his naked chest.

"That I relish the feel of your skin against mine?" I tease. "That I relish what we shared last night, and the night before that, and all the other nights?"

"Yes and yes," he grins. "It's nice to know that I make you happy." He roams my face with the back of his hand, his platinum eyes hypnotizing.

"Because that's what I want to do every single day. Everything I do is for you. I will do anything to make you happy, Anna. Anything."

"Anything?"

"Yes. Anything."

I bite my lip. "Hmm. . . Come to think of it, there *is* something I want. . ."

His brows curl. "What? What do you want?"

"I want. . . ," I lower my face and whisper to his ear, ". . . for Arion to have a playmate."

He slowly grins from ear to ear.

"Well, *that* can be arranged."

Then he proceeds to grant me what I want—and more.

*** THE END ***

ABOUT THE AUTHOR

Mayumi Cruz is a Filipino author writing diverse, cross-genre fiction with emotionally-charged and thought-provoking plots. Her books Chroma Hearts: A Psychological Thriller, and The Black Widow, have received awards and recognition. Some of Mayumi's writings have also appeared in Philippines Graphic and other online publications. To date, Mayumi has eighteen (18) published books, available online and in print.

Mayumi is also an artist, a website designer, a screenwriter, and a freelance editor. With degrees in Economics and Educational Management, she lives in the Philippines with her husband and three sons.

Website:
www.mayumi-cruz.com

Facebook:
https://www.facebook.com/MayumiCruzAuthorPage/

OTHER BOOKS BY MAYUMI CRUZ

Fantasy
MANANANGGAL IN THE CITY:
THE TIE THAT BINDS

Fantasy Suspense
IONE: A SEA WITCH'S TALE
AQUOSVEGNA: THE TRIDENT OF POWER

Dark Fantasy
THE INQUISITOR: A DYSTOPIAN DARK
FANTASY

Mythology Fantasy
THE BLACK WIDOW

Psychological Thriller
*2019 Best Published Story
CHROMA HEARTS

Speculative Fiction
DINNER FOR TWO AND OTHER SPECULATIVE
SHORT FICTION

Sci Fi Romance Thriller
FINDING KISMET

Romantic Suspense
THE BILLIONAIRE'S WIDOW

Romantic Comedy
IT'S NOT JUST SEMANTICS

Romantic Comedy Adventure

ESCAPE TO LOVE (Book 1, Meet the Petersons)
HUNTED HONEYMOON (Book 2, Meet the Petersons)

Women's Fiction
THE UNFAITHFUL WIFE

Children's Picture Book
RENZO'S RAINBOW

Journal
MY SMILE JOURNAL